PETER PANINI
and the Search for the Menehune

Written and Illustrated by
Stacey S. Kaopuiki

 HAWAIIAN ISLAND CONCEPTS

DEDICATION

This book is a gift from many hearts.
Through the time, efforts, encouragement
and aloha of many people, this book and
its characters have become a reality.

It is in this spirit and on behalf
of all these people that we dedicate
this book to the children of Hawaii.

Published by Hawaiian Island Concepts
P.O. Box 6280, Kahului, Maui, Hawaii 96732

Copyright Text and Illustrations © 1990
Hawaiian Island Concepts

First Printing: June, 1990
Second Printing: October, 1990

Book design by Wagstaff Graphic Design, Maui, Hawaii.

Library of Congress Catalogue Card Number: #90-81734

ISBN # 1-878498-00-2

Printed in Hong Kong.

Peter Panini and his dog Punahele looked forward to checking the mailbox each day.

One day Peter came running into the house full of excitement, and shouted, "Look Mom, there's a letter for me!" It was a letter from his cousin, Kalei, who lived on the island of Kaua'i.

"Aloha, Peter," wrote Kalei. *"Tutu* has told me about a group of mysterious little Hawaiian people called the *Menehune.*

"Very little is known about them and no one has ever found or seen one, but people believe they live here, near Uncle Kimo's house.

"See if you can visit me, because I am going to search for these little people . . . I am going to find a *Menehune!*

Aloha,
Kalei"

"Who are the *Menehune,* Mom?" asked Peter.

"The *Kupuna* say that they are very little people, kind of like Hawaiian elves. Strong and skilled, the *Menehune* build and repair the great stone walls throughout Hawaii. They also say that the *Menehune* are very *kolohe* and like to play tricks on people."

"Do you believe in the *Menehune,* Mom?" asked Peter.

"I haven't made up my mind yet, Peter. But maybe you, Kalei
and Punahele can find one and help me make up my mind."

"Mom, does that mean that we can go to Kauaʻi and search for
the *Menehune*?" asked Peter.

"Yes, you and Punahele may go."

As Peter packed his bag, he thought about the many adventures that he and Kalei had shared.

But to search for and find a *Menehune* was surely going to be the most exciting adventure of them all!

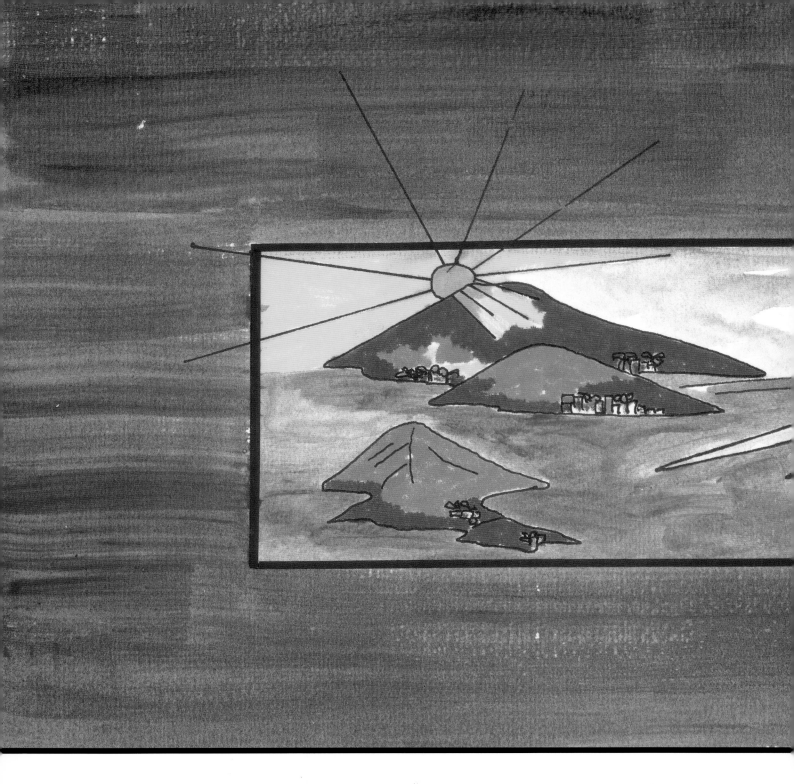

Soon, Peter and Punahele were high above the Hawaiian Islands.

The search for the *Menehune* was on!

When they arrived on Kaua'i, Peter and Punahele were happy to see Kalei again. . . .

Uncle Kimo's house sat along the banks of the Huleia River and was always a fun place to be. From many Hawaiian legends told by Uncle Kimo, Peter and Kalei learned about the mysterious *Menehune.*

It was only at night, when it was hard to be seen, that the *Menehune* would come out to work.

But before the morning sun would rise, when they heard the first rooster crow, the *Menehune* would silently disappear into the forest.

"Have you ever seen a *Menehune,* Uncle Kimo?" asked Kalei.

"No, I have not," said Uncle Kimo with a smile. "At least not yet. But you have come to the right place to look for them, for not far from here is the *Menehune* Fishpond.

"This large fishpond is said to have been built in just one night by the *Menehune* for a prince and princess of Kaua'i.

"The old Hawaiians called this place the Alakoko Fishpond, but it is now well known as the *Menehune* Fishpond.

"It is called this because the people of Kaua'i believe that the *Menehune* not only built the fishpond, but that they still live there and care for it.

"It is there that you will have the best chance of finding a *Menehune*."

"This trail will lead you to the *Menehune* Fishpond," said Uncle Kimo.

"Remember, you must look very carefully if you are ever to find the *Menehune* of Alakoko Fishpond.

"Good luck, Peter and Kalei. Be back by noon tomorrow."

Full of adventure and high spirits, Peter, Kalei and Punahele started off, following the path to the fishpond.

The great search for the *Menehune* had begun!

They started the search quickly, fighting their way through the thick brush that grew around the fishpond.

They looked high and low, between large rocks and under fallen branches.

But in the thick brush, they found no *Menehune*.

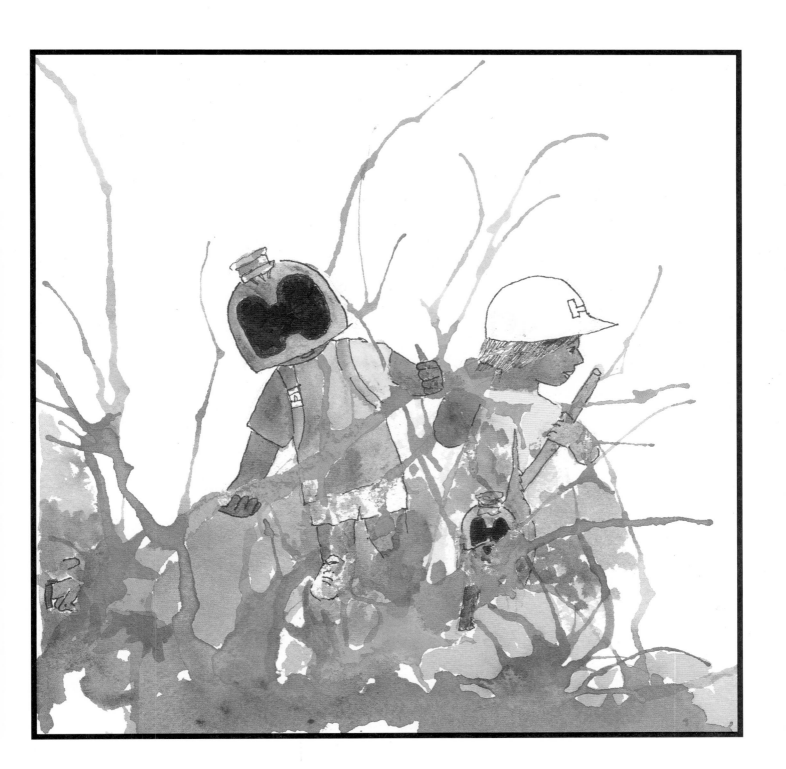

They climbed into the old taro patches and were swallowed up in a sea of green leaves.

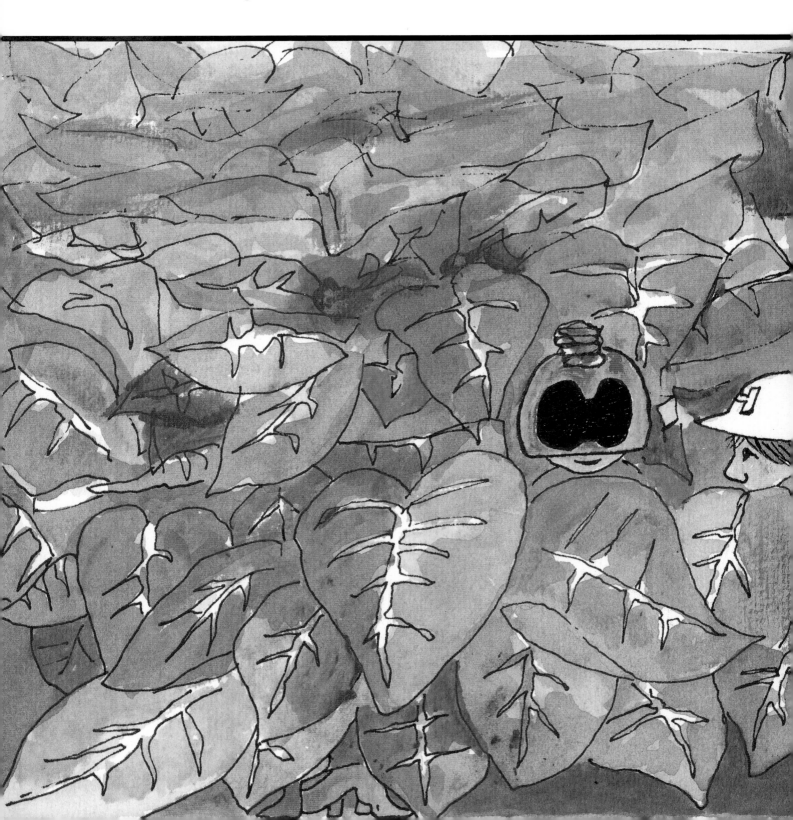

They looked over, searched under and crawled between the taro leaves.

But in the old taro patches, they found no *Menehune.*

They climbed up the highest of the great stone walls that lined the fishpond. From high above the fishpond they could see all around them.

They searched carefully, as far as they could see.

But from the great stone walls, they saw no *Menehune.*

They wandered far into the great *lauhala* forest and climbed the tallest trees.

They looked up between the prickly leaves and searched between the tangled roots.

But even in the great *lauhala* forest, they found no *Menehune.*

Into the dark night they searched, knowing that it was only at night that the *Menehune* would work.

They walked through the forest, past the taro patches and around the fishpond.

But on this night, even with their flashlights, they found no *Menehune.*

Tired and worn, the two adventurers made their way to their camp and snuggled into their sleeping bags.

"We've looked everywhere today, but we found no *Menehune* ... not even a sign. Do you think there really are *Menehune?*" asked Kalei.

"I don't think so," said a sleepy Peter Panini. "I think someone made them up."

"Yeah, me too," replied Kalei. "I think the *Menehune* are make-believe."

Soon they were fast asleep under a starry, starry sky.

Early the next morning, the disappointed band of adventurers packed and made their way back along the trail.

"Look!" said Kalei. "There's a crack in the stone wall and all the water from the fishpond is running out! What should we do?"

"We've got to fix the *puka!*" said Peter. "If we don't, all the water will be lost."

"If we do that, we won't make it back to Uncle Kimo's by noon," answered Kalei.

"He'll understand. Besides the *Menehune* are supposed to repair these walls, but we know that they don't exist. So if we don't fix the *puka,* who will?" asked Peter.

"You're right," said Kalei. "So let's get started!"

They both worked hard moving the heavy stones back into place. Then they packed the smaller cracks with little stones and mud until finally the water stopped.

"Alright, we're finished!" exclaimed Peter.

"Let's go, said Kalei. We'd better hurry before Uncle Kimo starts to worry about us."

Along the way home they entered a small clearing.

"Look, Peter!" shouted Kalei, pointing ahead.

There, on the soft wet ground, were a pair of tiny footprints that led towards a large rock. Excitedly, they followed the tracks, hoping to find who had made them.

The footprints ended at the large rock, as if the person who had made them had suddenly vanished.

Looking at the rock, Peter and Kalei saw a message written upon it:

Aloha, Peter, Kalei and Punahele,
We, the Menehune *of Alakoko Fishpond wish to say* mahalo *for fixing the crack in the old stone wall.*

We would have had to wait until nightfall before we could have come out to repair the wall. But by then much of the water in the fishpond would have been lost.

Because you stopped to fix the wall, you have saved the Alakoko Fishpond.

Although you searched very hard trying to find us, we were never far away. You will always be true friends of the Menehune.

May you always walk in peace and may your life be filled with rainbows.
Aloha,
The Menehune *of*
Alakoko Fishpond

"The *Menehune* of the fishpond really do exist," shouted Kalei.

"We've got to show Uncle Kimo the message that was left for us," said Peter excitedly.

"Let's go!"

But before they had taken a step, a small, very dark cloud drifted over the large rock and began to rain.

Peter and Kalei watched helplessly as the words, which had been written with mud, began to melt and run away.

Water and dirt started to fill the little footprints until they, too, blended with the earth. Everything had disappeared.

Suddenly, the most brilliant rainbow that they had ever seen appeared before them.

It was a rainbow they not only saw, but felt.

The red was as bright as the feather cloaks of the Hawaiian Alii.

The yellow shown like the sun.

The green was like the deep forest of the cool mountain valleys.

And the blue and purple melted into each other to remind them of the sea.

The rainbow was a gift for them and they watched quietly until it, too, disappeared.

Then, they walked off in silence, each lost in his own thoughts.

"Without proof, no one will believe what we've seen," said Kalei.

"Yeah, I guess this will have to be our own little secret," replied Peter. "But maybe it's better that things turned out the way they did."

"What do you mean?" asked Kalei.

"Well, what if a lot of other people had seen the message and the little footprints that we saw?" answered Peter. "Who knows what would happen then? Some people would probably destroy the forest and even the fishpond trying to find the *Menehune*. And if they ever found one, they would probably put him in a cage where he wouldn't be happy at all."

"Yeah, I know what you mean," said Kalei. "But...I still wish we had seen a *Menehune.*"

"Me too," said Peter.

HAVE *YOU* SEEN A *MENEHUNE?*

GLOSSARY

ALI'I: Royalty; kings, queens, chiefs, princes, princesses.

KIMO: The Hawaiian name for James.

KOLOHE: Rascal or mischievous.

KUPUNA: Respected elder; a person with great wisdom and knowledge.

LAUHALA: Pandanus tree; used to make mats.

MĀKINI: A Hawaiian gourd mask; this is the helmet worn by Peter Panini and his dog Punahele.

MENEHUNE: Legendary race of small people who worked at night, building fish ponds, roads, temples; like Hawaiian elves.

PUKA: A hole, opening, crack, or break.

PUNAHELE: A favorite one; Punahele was Peter's favorite dog.

TARO: The plant from which poi is made.

TUTU: Grandparents.